BUG ON THE RUG

By Sophia Gholz

Illustrated by Susan Batori

Pug on a rug,

cozy and snug.

He's a rug-loving pug.
When along comes . . .

Bug—looking real smug.

Bug on the rug—
right next to Pug!

Pug growls and howls. Bug buzzes and scowls.

He might be small,
but Bug stands tall.

Bug tosses a stick.

Pug chases it quick.

Bug gives a shrug—

says, "Goodbye, Pug."

Bug on the rug,
cozy and snug.

He's a rug-loving bug.

When along comes . . .

Pug—with one mad mug.

Pug tugs the rug,
shaking off Bug.
"I was here first!"
RRR
RRR
RRRRR

Pug fights with Bug—over the rug.

When along comes . . .

Slug—right under Pug.

Pug slips on Slug,

knocks into Bug.

They *swoosh*.
They *slide*.

Then they collide—

Pug, Bug, and Slug,
heaped on the rug.

"Rug-stealing bug!"

"Bug-shaking pug!"

Slug's stuck in between.
"You're both being mean."

Pug and Bug stop.
Tears start to drop.

“He is the hound
that smashed my mound.

Without a home,
I had to roam.”

Bizzle.
Bizzle.

Bzzz!
Bzzz!

Bug starts to wail.

Pug tucks his tail,
rethinks his day:

1. He went to play.

2. Took a long stroll.
DIRT STREET 5
3. Dug a deep hole—
GASP!

"I wrecked your mound—
I'm a bad hound!"
Whimper.
Whimper.
Waaa!
Waaa!

“I apologize!” Pug sniffles and cries.

Bug dries his eyes.
"Me too." He sighs.

"You didn't know.
I guess I'll go."

But then . . .

looking so wise,
Slug says, “Hey, guys,

you've cleared the air.
How 'bout you share?"

Pug and Bug stare.

"I think that's fair."

"I'll let you stay . . .
if you will play!"

"Group hug!"

sings Slug.

"And we're **ALL** snug."

LICK!

Pug, Bug, and Slug—fun on the rug!

He's a bug-loving pug.

He's a pug-loving bug.

When along comes . . .

Cat!